Kitty's magic

Star the Little Farm Cat

Ella Moonheart

illustrated by Dave Williams

BLOOMSBURY
CHILDREN'S BOOKS

NEW YORK   LONDON   OXFORD   NEW DELHI   SYDNEY

BLOOMSBURY CHILDREN'S BOOKS
Bloomsbury Publishing Inc., part of Bloomsbury Publishing Plc
1385 Broadway, New York, NY 10018

BLOOMSBURY, BLOOMSBURY CHILDREN'S BOOKS, and the Diana logo
are trademarks of Bloomsbury Publishing Plc

First published in Great Britain in July 2017 by Bloomsbury Publishing Plc
Published in the United States of America in June 2018 by Bloomsbury Children's Books
www.bloomsbury.com

Bloomsbury books may be purchased for business or promotional use. For information on bulk
purchases please contact Macmillan Corporate and Premium Sales Department at
specialmarkets@macmillan.com

Library of Congress Cataloging-in-Publication Data
Names: Moonheart, Ella, author.
Title: Star the little farm cat / by Ella Moonheart.
Description: New York : Bloomsbury, 2018. | Series: Kitty's magic ; 4
Summary: While visiting her aunt and uncle's farm, Kitty uses her ability to transform into
a cat to find out why her cousin, Max, is so unfriendly and helps with a mouse problem.
Identifiers: LCCN 2017050581
ISBN 978-1-68119-391-5 (paperback) • ISBN 978-1-68119-703-6 (hardcover)
ISBN 978-1-68119-392-2 (e-book)
Subjects: | CYAC: Cats—Fiction. | Shapeshifting—Fiction. | Magic—Fiction. |
Farm life—England—Fiction. | Japanese—England—Fiction. | England—Fiction.
Classification: LCC PZ7.1.M653 St 2018 | DDC [E] —dc23
LC record available at https://lccn.loc.gov/2017050581

Typeset by RefineCatch Limited, Bungay, Suffolk
Printed and bound in the U.S.A. by Berryville Graphics Inc., Berryville, Virginia
2 4 6 8 10 9 7 5 3 1 (paperback)
2 4 6 8 10 9 7 5 3 1 (hardcover)

To find out more about our authors and books visit www.bloomsbury.com
and sign up for our newsletters.

Kitty's magic

Star the Little Farm Cat

Kitty's Magic

Star the Little Farm Cat

Chapter 1

"Just one more sleep until my trip!" said Kitty Kimura. "I hope I like Aunt Wendy's farm."

Kitty's grandma looked at her. "I can tell you're a little bit nervous, Kitty," she said gently. "But I'm sure you'll love it at Strawberry Lane Farm. It's just beautiful!"

It was the start of the summer

vacation, and Kitty was helping her grandma at the family's shop on Willow Street. Kitty's parents were on a trip to Japan, where her dad and her grandma came from. They were buying lots of supplies for the shop, which sold special Japanese things.

Kitty missed them, but it was fun spending time with Grandma. Tomorrow, though, she was leaving for Strawberry Lane Farm, where Aunt Wendy and Uncle Greg lived. A real farm! Kitty's mom had told her it had lots of cows and horses, coops full of chickens, and a huge meadow dotted with strawberries, which gave the farm its pretty name. It was several hours away by train, and Kitty had never been there before. She'd never been away on her own before, either.

"You'll only be away for two nights, and Aunt Wendy and Uncle Greg will take very good care of you," Grandma went on. "Your cousin Max will be there too. I bet you'll be best friends right away. You're going to have a lovely time."

Kitty nodded, but she still felt a little bit uncertain. She *was* looking forward to seeing Strawberry Lane Farm, and to seeing Max again—but it all felt so far away from home, from Grandma, and from her best friend, Jenny, who Kitty usually saw every single day of the summer holidays.

Grandma smiled at Kitty, her eyes

twinkling. "I know what will cheer you up," she said. "Strawberry Lane Farm has lots of animals—including a cat!"

"Really?" Kitty's eyes lit up, and she grinned at Grandma. "I've never met a farm cat before. I think I *will* like Strawberry Lane Farm!"

Once they'd closed the shop that evening, Kitty asked Grandma if she could go out for a while.

"Of course, Kitty," Grandma replied. "I know you have a special friend to say goodbye to! Don't stay out too late, though. Remember, you've got a long journey tomorrow."

Kitty grinned. She'd already said goodbye to Jenny earlier that day.

Grandma was talking about another friend—a four-legged one. She gave Grandma a kiss on the cheek, then raced into the backyard. She glanced around quickly, to make sure that none of the neighbors was in sight. Then she reached for the silver pendant hanging around her neck, which had a picture of a cat engraved on it. Quietly, she recited the magic words.

"*Human hands to kitten paws,*
Human fingers, kitten claws."

Kitty closed her eyes and waited. Suddenly, a fizzing feeling swept through her toes, then into her feet and up her legs. Kitty grinned as the bubbling, tickling sensation whooshed through her whole body. No matter how many times it happened, Kitty never quite got used to how strange it felt!

When the feeling faded away, Kitty opened her eyes and looked around. Suddenly, the oak tree and the play-house at the end of the yard looked ten times bigger. Although it was twilight

and the yard was dim, Kitty could see every blade of grass and every flower petal vividly. Her nose filled with the beautiful scent of Grandma's lavender and rosebushes, and her ears picked up the faintest noises from the other side of the yard: the buzzing of a bee and the chattering of a line of tiny ants. Kitty's senses were more powerful for a magical reason—she had turned into a small black cat!

Being able to turn into a cat was Kitty's big secret. The only other person who knew was Grandma— because she had the same special ability too. It was Grandma who had given Kitty her necklace and taught her the magic words. Grandma had also introduced Kitty to the Cat Council, which was a nighttime meeting of all the cats in the neighborhood. Kitty even had a special role in the Cat Council: she was the Guardian. This meant cats could come to her with problems or questions, and she would try to help them.

Kitty loved her secret life as a cat, although it had taken her a while to get used to having a tail! Her favorite thing to do in cat form was explore the town late at night—while all her human family and friends were fast asleep—with her new cat friends for company.

Kitty stretched her furry black legs and flexed her paws, then leaped onto the backyard fence and trotted along it. As she walked, her tail swayed from side to side, helping her to balance. She was heading for her best friend Jenny's house—where her best cat friend also lived.

"Hi, Misty!" Kitty meowed, jumping down into the backyard, where a small

silver tabby was curled up on Jenny's trampoline.

Misty sprang up when she saw Kitty, her blue eyes gleaming. The two cats bumped foreheads to say hello.

"Kitty! I'm so glad you came to see me. I thought you might have already left for your aunt's farm!" purred Misty.

"I wouldn't leave without saying goodbye, Misty. I'm leaving tomorrow," Kitty explained. "Grandma's taking me on the train after lunch. And guess what? There's a cat at the farm!"

"A farm cat! I've never met one of those before," Misty meowed excitedly. "I've never even been to a farm," she added. "I've only ever lived in a town. I wonder what it will be like."

Kitty purred thoughtfully. "I think it's going to be very big, with lots of grass and places to run around," she said. "Mom says Aunt Wendy and Uncle Greg have some black-and-white cows, some chickens, and a huge, scary-looking bull. I'm going to stay away from him! And I think there'll be lots of trees to climb."

"Climbing trees is my favorite. I wish I was going with you!" said Misty wistfully. "We'd have so much fun there together. But at least you'll have the farm cat to play with."

"I wish you were coming too! I'll tell you all about it as soon as I get back. I just hope the farm cat is friendly," said Kitty, a little anxiously.

Most of the cats she'd met since discovering her secret gift had been very nice, but not all. Just like people, Kitty had found that cats had very different personalities!

Chapter 2

The next day, Grandma and Kitty caught a train into the city, then another, smaller train into the countryside where Aunt Wendy and Uncle Greg lived. Kitty watched out the window as the tall buildings and busy traffic turned into wide open fields dotted with sheep and cows and the occasional scarecrow. She smiled at Grandma, but her tummy felt as though it were full of butterflies.

Finally, the train pulled into a little station. "Kitty, this is our stop!" said Grandma, reaching for Kitty's suitcase. The butterflies in Kitty's tummy fluttered even more.

As Kitty and Grandma stepped off the train, Kitty heard a friendly voice calling her name. "Kitty, over here!"

Aunt Wendy came running toward them, waving. She looked just like Kitty's mom, with the same wavy blond hair and freckles. She was dressed in a T-shirt, jeans, and sturdy green rubber boots that were blotchy with mud. Kitty hoped she'd packed the right sort of clothes for a farm. She hadn't really been sure what to bring.

"It's so good to see you both!" said Aunt Wendy, hugging Kitty and Grandma. "Kitty, you remember Max, don't you? You two are about the same age, although it's been a while since you've seen one another."

Kitty turned and saw her cousin, who was standing a little awkwardly nearby, his hands stuffed into his pockets. He had messy sandy-brown hair that fell into his eyes. Kitty smiled and said, "Hi, Max."

Max just nodded and looked away. "Can we go home now, Mom?" he muttered.

"Maybe he's shy, Kitty. Don't worry, he'll warm up to you," Grandma whispered, as they followed Aunt Wendy and Max to the car.

Aunt Wendy drove them back to the farm. Kitty thought the farmhouse looked very welcoming with its white walls and brightly painted blue front door. Two tall apple trees stood on either side of the house, their branches bobbing in the breeze as if they were waving hello. There was a muddy yellow tractor parked to one side of the house. Beyond it, Kitty could see a row of wooden chicken coops on tall legs, a barn, and a huge field dotted with strawberries.

There were lots of funny smells in the air, and Kitty wrinkled her nose, imagining how strong they'd be if she were smelling them with her cat nose! As she did so, she caught her cousin Max frowning at her. The butterflies in her tummy started fluttering again. She hoped he wasn't going to be this grumpy for the whole of her stay.

A smiling man with a beard came out of the farmhouse, holding something small and furry in his arms. "Hello, Kitty!" he called. "We've all been looking forward to your visit. We've got a new member of the family for you to meet."

"Hi, Uncle Greg!" said Kitty. She stepped forward and gasped in delight at the tiny, furry bundle he was carrying. "A puppy!"

"This is Daisy," explained Uncle Greg. "She's actually Max's puppy, isn't she, Max?"

Max nodded. "She's a border collie and she's six weeks old," he added. He

held out his arms and the puppy wriggled into them, licking his face excitedly.

"Max, I'm sure Kitty would love to pet Daisy," Aunt Wendy said.

Max sighed, but he let Kitty run her fingers over the puppy's silky fur. Daisy was black with a large patch of white on her chest and another on her head, and she wore a collar with a strawberry print. Kitty smiled as Daisy's little tail wagged eagerly.

"She likes you!" said Aunt Wendy, laughing.

"I bet you've never met a real farm dog before," said Max, looking at Kitty.

Kitty thought Max sounded a little

unfriendly, but she couldn't figure out why he didn't seem to like her. "No, I haven't," she admitted. "I really like dogs, though—although cats are my favorite."

"I remember your mom telling me that!" said Aunt Wendy, smiling. "Well, you're in luck, Kitty—we have a cat too. Star isn't a baby like Daisy, though. We've had him for years and years. He's even older than you and Max! You'll meet him tomorrow. He can usually be found in the barn, looking out for—"

"Mom!" Max interrupted. "Er, maybe we should take Kitty's suitcase inside."

Aunt Wendy gave Max a funny look,

then nodded. "Max is right. Let's get you inside, and I'll make everyone a nice cold drink."

"And then I'll be off to catch my train home," said Grandma.

Kitty's tummy wobbled a little as she stepped inside the farmhouse—but it was just as welcoming and cozy as it looked from the outside. It was very different from her own house, which was small, neat, and tidy. The kitchen was huge and rather messy, full of pots and pans that didn't match, with jars of wildflowers scattered around. The walls were covered in photographs, and Kitty smiled as she saw that lots of them were of her parents and herself.

"It feels like a very friendly house,

doesn't it?" Grandma whispered to Kitty as Aunt Wendy poured glasses of apple and strawberry juice for everyone. "You'll have a wonderful weekend here, Kitty."

Kitty had to admit that she liked Strawberry Lane Farm very much. But as Grandma finished her drink and said goodbye to everyone, Kitty felt a little bit nervous again. Would she manage to fall asleep in a strange bed tonight? Would she be able to find her way around the farm? And what if Star the farm cat turned out to be grumpy, like her cousin Max?

As she hugged Grandma goodbye, Kitty decided to leave turning into a cat until after she'd met Star as a human.

I'll get to know my way around the farm tomorrow, in the daytime, she thought. *Then, if Star seems nice, I'll turn into a cat—and get to know him properly!*

Chapter 3

A loud squawking woke Kitty the next morning. Her eyes flew open and she sat straight up in bed, blinking. As she looked around the unfamiliar bedroom, it took a few moments for her to remember she was at Strawberry Lane Farm.

The noise rang out again. Kitty climbed out of bed, ran to the window, and looked outside. A large, plump bird with a bright red crest on top of its head was strutting around in front of the chicken coops. "A rooster," Kitty whispered.

As she watched, Uncle Greg strode into the yard carrying a basket. He glanced up and waved at her. "Morning, Kitty!" he called. "Did you sleep well? Why don't you get dressed and run down here—you can help me collect some eggs for breakfast."

Kitty threw on her jeans, top, and sandals, and went downstairs. She stepped out of the front door and into the farmyard. She'd only taken a few steps when she heard a loud squelching

noise and felt something cold ooze over her toes. "Oh, yuck," she said, laughing and looking down. "Mud!"

"Ah, yes. I'm afraid you can't walk anywhere on Strawberry Lane Farm without getting muddy," explained Uncle Greg. "It's everywhere. Your sandals are lovely, Kitty, but they're going to get ruined very quickly. Wait there a moment, and I'll go and grab you some boots. You and Max must be about the same size."

Kitty nodded, and stood waiting in the mud as Uncle Greg dashed inside. She heard a snicker behind her and turned to see Max walking past with Daisy at his heels. Her cheeks flushed and she glared after Max. Why was he being so unfriendly?

Uncle Greg soon came back with a pair of blue rubber boots, which he helped Kitty put on. "We'll put your muddy sandals in the sun to dry," Uncle Greg said, pegging them on the clothesline that ran across the front of the farmhouse. "Now let's go and find our breakfast!"

Uncle Greg showed Kitty how to shoo the chickens out of their coops and carefully feel around in the straw for any eggs that had been laid since yesterday. Kitty was in charge of placing the eggs gently in the basket, making sure she didn't drop or crush any. "I think that's all of them," she said, feeling around one last time in the final coop.

"That means it's time to eat!" replied Uncle Greg.

Together, they carried the basket into the kitchen, and Uncle Greg began frying the eggs and slicing bread for toast. Aunt Wendy had already set the table, and when Kitty sat down she saw that she had been given a plate with tiny black cats dancing around the edge. Breakfast was delicious, and Aunt Wendy and Uncle Greg chatted to Kitty about her school and friends. But next to her, Max didn't say a word.

I really wish Jenny was here, she thought to herself. *Or Misty!* Thinking of her best friends made home feel very far away, and suddenly everything in the farmhouse felt extra strange and unfamiliar.

Aunt Wendy seemed to be able to tell that Kitty was feeling unhappy, and she gave her a warm smile. "I know! Why don't you go and find Star, Kitty? Uncle Greg and I have to pick some strawberries to sell at the market tomorrow, but Max will show you Star's favorite spot, in the barn."

"Okay!" said Kitty, brightening up. *Maybe meeting a cat will make me feel more at home*, she told herself.

After the breakfast things were cleared away, Kitty followed Max across the farmyard toward the barn. As they drew closer, Kitty saw Star sprawled in a patch of sunlight in front of the barn doors. He was an old tomcat with long, straggly whiskers and several black- and rust-colored patches on his body. One of the patches looked like a five-pointed star. "So that's where his name comes from!" Kitty said, pointing to it. She thought

she caught a glimpse of a smile on Max's face, but then he just nodded and turned away. "I have things to do," he told her. "See you later."

Kitty frowned as Max stomped off. Just what had she done to upset him? She couldn't work it out!

"At least *you* seem friendly, Star," she said, stroking his soft, warm fur. Star purred and rubbed his head against her hand. Kitty grinned. Meeting a cat *had* made her feel better!

That gives me an idea, she thought, glancing around. Max was out of sight now, and Aunt Wendy and Uncle Greg were busy in the strawberry patch. Kitty decided to take her chance. Clutching her pendant in one hand, she closed her eyes and whispered the special words.

The strange tickling, bubbling sensation rushed around her body. She felt her arms and legs shrinking and the prickle of her fur and whiskers appearing and heard a shocked meow. When she opened her eyes again, she was nose to nose with Star, who was staring at her in amazement.

"I've never seen a human do that before!" the old tomcat meowed. "I'm Star. Who are you?"

"I'm Kitty," Kitty said, offering her head for Star to bump. "I'm Max's cousin. But Max doesn't know I can turn into a cat. It's a secret!"

"Amazing!" Star purred. "Well, Kitty, welcome to Strawberry Lane Farm!"

Kitty explained that she'd never been to a farm before. Immediately, Star offered to show her around. Kitty could tell that the old cat was very proud of his home.

"Let's head to the meadow over

there," Star suggested, pointing with a front paw.

Kitty glanced around once more to check that none of her human family were close by. She knew that if they spotted a strange black cat on the farm, they might chase her away! But there was still no sign of her aunt and uncle, and her clever cat ears could hear Max calling to Daisy a long way away, so she knew he was busy.

They padded across the farmyard and Star showed Kitty a gap in the fence for them to jump through. Grazing in the meadow were two huge horses. One was a slender chestnut, and one was black and rather plump. When they saw the cats they lifted their heads, snorted their big nostrils curiously, and trotted toward them.

Kitty had never met a horse in her cat form before, and was amazed by how enormous they seemed. She stared up at their powerful legs, their long necks and their huge heads. As they flicked their shaggy tails and shuffled their heavy, muddy hoofs closer, Kitty shrank back a little. But Star nudged her forward encouragingly. "This is Holly, and this is Seamus," he told her. "Don't worry, Kitty. They're very big but they're very friendly!"

The chestnut horse, Holly, gave a kind whinny and lowered her head right down to the grass, so that she and Kitty were face to face. She had shiny

black eyes with long lashes and a pink, velvety nose. "It's nice to meet you!" she neighed.

"Any friend of Star's is a friend of ours," said the plump black horse, Seamus. "Er, I don't suppose you've seen any carrots lying around?" he added hopefully. "Or sugar lumps? They'd be even better. I'm starving!"

Holly rolled her eyes. "Seamus, you're always hungry," she tutted.

Kitty couldn't believe it. "I didn't know I could understand other animals!" she meowed. "I thought it was just other cats! I've never even tried talking to other animals before. Can all animals understand each other, Star?"

"Oh yes!" Star purred. "That's what

makes living on a farm so much fun. There are always so many other animals to talk to. As well as Holly and Seamus, there are the cows and the bull, Bruce. He looks scary but he's really friendly. Then there are the chickens, the ducks, and the saddleback pigs."

"What about Daisy?" asked Kitty, remembering the newest animal at Strawberry Lane Farm.

Star looked surprised. "Why would I want to talk to a dog? Never liked dogs, never will. Cats and dogs are just too different. Everyone knows that."

Kitty nodded. She'd spent enough time with the Cat Council to understand that cats and dogs were rarely friends.

"Puppies might be smaller, but they're just as bad," added Star, with a shudder. "Anyway—let's go and say hello to the ducks next. Their pond is just this way."

"Bye, Kitty!" called Holly.

"If either of you do find any sugar lumps, just let me know," added Seamus with a hopeful grin.

As Kitty padded after Star, she noticed the older cat was a little slow and unsteady on his paws.

"I'm not as quick as I used to be, I'm afraid," Star meowed. "I used to be the fastest cat around. Shooting Star, the other animals used to call me, but my poor old legs get so tired these days."

As he spoke, Kitty caught a flash of

movement out of the corner of her eye. Something small and brown with tiny, beady black eyes had darted across the field toward the barn. Her ears suddenly pricked up and she felt the fur on the back of her neck tingle. There was a funny smell in the air too, and her nose twitched. "Star, what was that?" she asked.

Star crouched low, his eyes wide. "Mouse!" he hissed. "It'll be looking for food to steal. Quick, Kitty. Let's chase it away!"

Star leapt after the mouse and Kitty followed. But as they ran, Kitty saw tiny brown shapes darting all around. There wasn't just *one* mouse to chase, there were at least ten! She raced after the nearest one, but it disappeared into a crack in the barn wall. Another fled into a hay bale. As quickly as they had appeared, the mice disappeared.

"There are so many of them!" meowed Kitty. "And they're so fast!"

The old tomcat came panting to a halt. "I can't keep up with them all, Kitty," he said. "My eyesight and sense

of smell are as good as they've ever been, but my legs keep letting me down." He gave a sorrowful meow. "Keeping mice away from the farm is supposed to be one of my main jobs. Strawberry Lane Farm never had a mouse problem when I was younger and faster."

As Star's whiskers drooped, Kitty knew immediately what she had to do. Star was a cat with a problem, and she was a Guardian. So, as a Guardian, she would try to solve it. She would try to help Star get the mouse problem under control. The question was—how?

Chapter 4

As they went back over to the barn, Star stretched and yawned, showing his pointed teeth. "All that running around has tired me out," he purred. "Time for my cat nap. Perhaps you could come and visit me later, Kitty?"

"Of course," Kitty replied.

Star curled up in the patch of sunshine

where Kitty had found him earlier. As he closed his eyes, Kitty heard an excited bark and the clatter of paws racing across the farmyard. It was Daisy!

Quickly, Kitty darted behind a nearby watering can and peeped around. She knew that if Daisy was here, Max could be close behind—especially if he heard her barking. Kitty couldn't let him spot her!

As Kitty watched, the little puppy jumped on Star playfully, her tail wagging at full speed. "Let's play!" she yapped.

Star's eyes flew open and he leaped away from Daisy, his back arched and his fur standing on end. "How many

times do I have to tell you?" the old tomcat hissed. "Leave me alone!" Then he stalked off, muttering angrily.

Kitty glanced back at Daisy. The tiny puppy was gazing after Star sadly, her ears drooping and her tail hanging still.

Poor Daisy! Kitty thought. *I want to try to cheer her up—but she's a dog! I'm not sure if I'm supposed to help other animals, especially dogs—they can cause so much trouble for cats. I wish the Cat Council was here so I could ask them their advice.*

Kitty made a decision. Even though she knew it was very unusual for cats and dogs to mix and she wasn't sure she was doing the right thing, she decided to try to make friends with the little puppy. Quickly checking Max was still nowhere in sight, she slipped out of her hiding place and trotted toward Daisy. The puppy's tail started wagging again. "Yippee, another cat!" she barked. She bounded forward, sniffing Kitty's face curiously. Kitty took a step back. Suddenly, Daisy looked anxious. "You're not mad at me too, are you? Star gets mad at me a lot."

"No, I'm not mad at you," Kitty meowed.

Daisy gave a yelp of relief. "Where did you come from? I thought there was only one cat here."

"My name's Kitty. I'm Max's cousin. I met you yesterday—when I was a human," Kitty explained. "But I'm able to turn into a cat. It's a big secret."

Daisy's eyes widened and she gave Kitty another sniff. "I knew there was something strange about you!" she yapped. "You smell like a cat—but like a human too!"

When Daisy had finished sniffing her, Kitty asked, "Are you okay, Daisy? You seemed really sad just now. I'm sure Star didn't mean to upset you."

"I just wish Star would play with me, but he never wants to. He won't even talk to me," Daisy snuffled sadly. "I miss the rest of my litter. I had lots of

brothers and sisters to play with before I came here."

"You're homesick!" Kitty meowed. "I understand, Daisy. I'm a bit homesick too. Things here are different from how I thought they'd be. I thought my cousin Max would be friendly and show me around, but I don't think he likes me."

Daisy's brown eyes lit up and her tail gave a sudden wag. "Max is my favorite person in the whole world! I heard him talking to his mom about you!" she woofed. "It was just before you arrived. He said you wouldn't like Strawberry Lane Farm. He thought you'd look down your nose at everything because you're from a town, where everything is clean and tidy—and there isn't mud everywhere!"

Kitty stared at Daisy. "Wait a minute—you can understand what humans say? I thought it was only cats who could do that."

"All dogs can understand people," Daisy explained. "All other animals too! At least, all the animals I've met can."

Kitty thought about what Daisy had just told her. "I can't believe Max thought I wouldn't like it here just because it's a little muddy!"

Daisy nodded eagerly. "And he said you'd be frightened by the mice. I think he was a bit embarrassed about it. He didn't want you to know how many mice there are here."

Kitty opened her mouth to reply, but Daisy caught sight of something behind her. "There's one now!" she barked excitedly. "Let's chase it, Kitty!"

Kitty whirled around as one of the mice that she and Star had chased crept out of its hiding place. As Daisy bounded toward it, barking madly, it shot around the corner of the house. Daisy ran after it, still yapping, and it raced out of the yard and off across the fields.

Kitty was about to follow Daisy— but then Max came around the corner.

"Daisy, what's going on?" he called, chasing after his puppy. "Slow down, slow down! Where's Kitty? I thought she was out here."

Max looked around—and spotted Kitty, who had started taking tiny steps backward, desperately searching for a place to hide. "Hey!" Max called. "Where did that black cat come from?"

Chapter 5

Kitty ran as fast as her paws could carry her. Grandma had explained that if any person ever discovered her secret, her special gift would be lost forever. She couldn't let Max find out that *she* was the little black cat!

She darted onto a wheelbarrow that was leaning against the farmhouse and sprang through an open window. As she padded upstairs and slipped into her bedroom, she heard Max run inside the house.

Quickly, Kitty closed her eyes and whispered:

"*Kitten paws to human toes,*

Kitten whiskers, human nose."

That had been close! Kitty transformed back into a girl just as Max reached the landing outside her bedroom. She stepped out of the room and saw a look of surprise on her cousin's face.

"Oh!" Max said. "It's you. I didn't know you were in here. I was looking for a cat—a little black one. It ran inside the house. Have you seen it?"

Kitty's heart was beating so loudly

she was sure Max would be able to hear it. "Er, no," she answered, hoping she wasn't blushing. "No cats in here."

"Huh?" Max looked around, puzzled. "I was sure it ran up this way. Maybe it went out through the back door." He shot Kitty a glance. "We always leave it open. You probably don't leave your

doors open like that, do you? Living in a town."

Kitty remembered what Daisy had told her—that Max had been sure Kitty wouldn't like how different the countryside was from the town. Quickly she replied, "No, but I think it's much nicer to be able to leave it open."

Max looked surprised.

"Maybe we'll see that little black cat later," Kitty said with a smile. "I love how many animals there are here. You're so lucky to live here, Max."

For the rest of the day, Max was a bit friendlier to Kitty. When they sat down to eat dinner that evening, he even asked her if she wanted to go out and see Holly and Seamus with him later on.

"I'd love to!" said Kitty. But as she spoke, there was a loud grumble of thunder from outside.

"You might have to wait until tomorrow to take Kitty to see the horses, I'm afraid," said Aunt Wendy, standing up from the table. "It sounds like we've got a big storm coming. I'd better go and make sure all the animals are inside."

"And I'll go bring Daisy in," said Uncle Greg, as the little dog began barking from the farmyard. "Animals can get very anxious during storms, especially young animals like Daisy," he explained to Kitty.

"It's lucky we picked all those straw-berries today!" Aunt Wendy said, pulling on her raincoat. "The straw-berry patch will be a muddy mess tomorrow."

"Yes, I just hope the mice don't nibble the berries overnight." Uncle Greg said. "I stored the baskets in the barn and covered them with a few sheets, but the little pests seem to be able to get into anything. If they manage to get into the baskets, all the straw-berries will be ruined. We won't be able to sell any!"

Aunt Wendy sighed. "They're getting worse every week. It's so annoying, Kitty. There are plenty of wild berries and seeds for them to nibble in the fields outside the farm, but they seem to prefer ours." She glanced at Star, who'd come into the kitchen to shelter from the rain. "Poor Star. He just can't keep up with them anymore."

Kitty saw the old cat's ears droop

sadly as he heard what his humans were saying. Her heart sank. Kitty knew that her aunt and uncle made money from selling goods from the farm, like strawberries, milk, and eggs. If the mice were spoiling their produce they wouldn't be able to sell it, and that would mean big problems for Strawberry Lane Farm.

Kitty frowned. This was even more serious than she had realized. But what could she do?

She decided she had to try to help Star protect the strawberries that night. She just hoped the storm would blow over!

Chapter 6

That night, when Kitty was sure that her aunt, uncle, and cousin were all asleep, she crept out of bed. Very quietly, she whispered the magic words and transformed into a cat. Then she nudged her bedroom door open with her furry forehead and padded downstairs.

"Star!" she whispered, trotting

through the hallway and into the kitchen. "Star, where are you?"

There was a crackle of thunder from outside. It was almost pitch black inside the house, but luckily her keen cat eyes could see every detail, so it didn't feel as scary.

"Over here, Kitty!" Star was standing by the cat flap in the front door. "I'm going to the barn!" he meowed quietly. "I need to protect the strawberries from the mice. You heard what my humans said. If the mice get to them, they'll be ruined!"

"I'll come too," Kitty said. She could hear the rain pattering hard against the windows and imagined how muddy it must be outside now. Secretly, she

really didn't want to go out in the storm—but she had to help her new friend.

Star nodded gratefully and pushed open the cat flap with one paw. But as he did so, there was another, even louder rumble of thunder, and a flash of bright lightning lit up the whole farmyard. Star and Kitty both gasped and jumped back, letting the cat flap swing shut again.

"The storm's right above us!" hissed Star.

Kitty realized her fur was standing on end. As a girl, she'd never minded storms—but as a cat, she felt terrified! Star was trembling too. How would they make it to the barn? She glanced around the hallway helplessly, and saw an umbrella stand in the corner. Suddenly, she had an idea.

"Star, I know what to do!" she said. "Wait there!"

She whispered the words to turn

herself back into a human, and closed her eyes. She heard a meow of surprise from Star as the strange, magical feeling spread through her claws and paws, around her body, and whooshed through her tail and the tips of her whiskers. When she opened her eyes, she was a girl again—and now the storm didn't feel too scary after all!

Star was staring up at Kitty, eagerly waiting to see what she would do next. Kitty grabbed Max's spare pair of boots from the shoe rack and pulled them on. Then she crouched down and carefully picked Star up. Holding him securely in one arm, she snatched an umbrella from the umbrella stand. "I'm going to carry

you to the barn, Star!" she whispered. "And I promise we'll stay dry!"

Holding the umbrella above them, Kitty opened the door and slipped outside. Lightning crackled in the sky as she ran to the barn, splashing through deep puddles. She rushed inside the barn, breathing a sigh of relief. "We made it, Star!" she cried, letting the cat drop down on to the ground. "And I'd better change back into a cat quickly—it looks like the mice are here!"

Kitty could see several tiny shapes darting around the boxes of strawberries that were stacked in the middle of the barn and covered with white sheets. As Star pounced, Kitty muttered the rhyme and transformed back into a cat. As soon as she had changed, her clever cat ears could hear squeaks and nibbling sounds, and her nose and whiskers twitched and tingled with the smell of mice. "Leave those strawberries alone!" she hissed in her scariest voice, leaping toward the nearest mouse.

But the mice were brave and fast—and there were just too many of them! Star and Kitty chased the mice around the barn until they were panting for breath, but the sneaky little creatures ducked into nooks and crannies in the barn walls, or stayed hidden between the strawberry boxes where the cats couldn't reach them. As Kitty and Star stopped for a second to rest, they heard the squeaking, chattering noises return.

"It's not working!" cried Star. "We just can't keep up with them all."

Kitty felt her heart sink. If the mice weren't chased away, Aunt Wendy and Uncle Greg's strawberries would be ruined! But what else could they try?

"Kitty! Star!"

Kitty whirled around as she heard a nervous bark behind her. "Daisy! What are you doing here?"

Chapter 7

Daisy stood at the barn door, her black-and-white fur dripping wet. She was shaking, and her big eyes were very wide. "I followed you," she yelped. "I heard you talking about the mice, and I wanted to help. But the storm was so scary! It took a little while before I felt brave enough to come after you!"

Star frowned at the puppy. "You came to help us?" he asked, puzzled.

Daisy nodded. "If you don't mind," the puppy added nervously.

Star looked uncertain, but Kitty nodded eagerly. "Thank you, Daisy!" she meowed.

"So what shall we do?" Daisy asked.

Kitty thought. "Well . . . earlier today, the mice ran away when you barked at them, Daisy. So maybe they don't like loud noises—just like we didn't like the storm!" She looked around the barn and her eyes lit up.

"There are lots of tools and pieces of equipment here. Why don't we try making a real racket with them? If we're noisy enough, we might scare them off!"

Kitty pointed a paw toward a row of heavy gardening tools that were lined up against the barn wall. "Daisy, you run around and bark as loudly as you can. Star and I can push those over. It will be even louder than the thunder!"

Star still looked a little unsure.

"Star, maybe you have some extra tips for Daisy?" Kitty said. "You've been catching mice for years, so you must know all the best tricks."

To her relief, the old tomcat nodded. "Daisy, try using your nose to sniff out the mice," he meowed. "If you know exactly where each mouse is hiding, you can bark and growl right by their hiding place."

Daisy's tail began wagging furiously. "This is fun!" she yelped.

Daisy raced in circles around the strawberries, sniffing for mice and yapping and growling fiercely whenever she found one. Kitty glanced anxiously toward the house, worried that Aunt

Wendy and Uncle Greg might hear the racket. But the storm was too noisy for anyone in the house to hear what was going on in the barn.

"Look, there!" whispered Star.

The first mouse had crept out from the stack of strawberries, disturbed by the loud noise. Kitty and Star ran toward the gardening tools and nudged them with their foreheads, springing away as they clattered noisily to the floor. With an angry squeak, the mouse rushed from the barn. A moment later, the rest of the mice followed! Kitty and Daisy chased after them, making sure that not a single mouse was left behind.

"And don't come back!" barked Daisy

as the last mouse fled. "Those strawberries aren't for you, remember!"

"It worked!" purred Star. "They're
all gone."

"Hooray!" cried Kitty. "We did it!"

"We make a good team!" Daisy
woofed happily.

Star chuckled and glanced at Daisy a
little shyly. "It's funny, I never thought
a cat and dog could have anything in
common," he admitted. "But we both
wanted to help our humans. Maybe
we're more alike than I realized! I'm
sorry I was so grumpy, Daisy."

Daisy's tail wagged happily. "I'm
glad I could help, Star!" she barked.
"And if the mice come back, maybe I
could help again?"

Kitty's eyes lit up. "That's it!" she said. "Daisy and Star—why don't you work together to keep the mice away? Star, you can't run very quickly anymore, but you've got lots of mouse-chasing experience, and your sense of smell and sight are still excellent. Daisy, you're new to chasing mice, but you're really fast, and you've got a noisy bark. If you were a team, the mice wouldn't stand a chance against you."

Star nodded. "You're right, Kitty!" he purred eagerly. "I could really do with the help."

"I'd love to be on your team, Star," yelped Daisy, her tail wagging.

Kitty smiled as Star and Daisy nuzzled

heads. "Right, we'd better get back inside the house before any of the humans wake up. And I'd better go to bed!"

Chapter 8

"Mom! Dad!" cried Max when he came downstairs the next morning. "Look at Star and Daisy!"

Kitty grinned as Aunt Wendy and Uncle Greg came and peered at the cozy spot in front of the oven. Star and Daisy were cuddled up together in a furry heap. Star was purring loudly, and Daisy's little tail was wagging.

"I've never seen them do that before," said Aunt Wendy, shaking her head. "I wonder what's changed."

Kitty wished she could tell them what had happened last night. She loved hearing them so excited about Star and Daisy's new friendship.

After breakfast, Uncle Greg stood up and said, "Right, better go and check

the strawberries. I just hope the mice didn't get them all."

Kitty and Max pulled on their boots and followed Uncle Greg out to the barn. The storm had finally passed and it was a sunny morning, though rainwater was still dripping from the apple trees and there were muddy puddles everywhere. As they went into the barn, Kitty kept a lookout for any mice that might have crept back in—but to her relief, she didn't spot one.

Uncle Greg pulled back one of the sheets that covered the strawberries and peered at the baskets one by one. Finally he shook his head. "Not a single berry has been nibbled. I can't believe it! I was sure they'd manage to get to them last night." His face broke into a smile. "Perhaps it was the storm that kept them away?"

"Or maybe it was Daisy!" suggested Kitty. "She's good at chasing mice—I saw her do it yesterday."

Max nodded. "Kitty's right. I've seen Daisy chasing them before too."

"Daisy *and* Star," Kitty added. "Star isn't as fast as Daisy, but together, I bet they make a really good mouse-chasing team."

"Do you know, I think you may be right," Uncle Greg said thoughtfully. "There *were* wet paw prints in the hallway this morning, so Daisy and Star must have been out in the storm last night." He chuckled. "Daisy and

Star—top mouse-chasing team. I like the sound of that! And it really would be a big help to the farm. Right, I'd better start loading the strawberries into the car, ready for the market."

"I'll help, Dad," offered Max.

"Me too!" said Kitty, picking up the nearest basket.

Max gave Kitty a shy smile as they walked through the farmyard with their baskets. "You know, I didn't think you'd like it here on the farm," he said. "I thought you'd hate the mud and the funny smells, and all the chores."

Kitty smiled at him. "I love it here!" And it was true. She hadn't felt home-sick for ages. She couldn't believe she'd be going home that afternoon—and although she was excited to go home, she felt a bit sad too. It had all gone so quickly. "Life on a farm is really different," she said, "but it's fun. Maybe I could come again, next break?" she suggested. "And you should visit me in town someday too!"

"I'd like that a lot!" replied Max.

Kitty's last day on the farm went by in a flash. Once all the strawberries had been loaded in the car, the family drove to the market to sell them. Max helped Uncle Greg collect the money from people, while Kitty handed out the baskets. The strawberries were so plump and delicious they sold out in no time.

When they got back to the farm, it was almost time for Kitty to go home. She went upstairs to pack her bag. When she came back down, Grandma had arrived.

Kitty ran to give her a big, tight hug. "Grandma, wait until I tell you everything that's happened!" she said.

"I'm looking forward to it, Kitty!" replied Grandma, her eyes twinkling. "Have you enjoyed yourself?"

"I've had the best time. I love it here!" said Kitty.

"And we've loved having you, Kitty!" said Aunt Wendy. "I do wish you were staying a bit longer!"

"Next time, you must stay for a week!" added Uncle Greg.

"I'd love that," Kitty replied.

"Me too," Max said with a grin.

"Would it be okay if I go and say goodbye to the animals?" Kitty asked.

"Of course," Grandma replied. "Our train doesn't leave for a while yet."

"Could I take a carrot for Seamus?" Kitty said, looking at the crate of freshly dug vegetables in the corner of the kitchen.

"Absolutely," Uncle Greg said, handing her a bunch. "That should keep him happy!"

"I'll come with you," Max said.

As he and Kitty made their way over to the door, Daisy trotted along happily behind them.

Chapter 9

As soon as Seamus spotted Kitty entering the meadow, he gave a whinny of delight and came trotting over.

"I'm really going to miss you, Seamus," Kitty said, feeding him one of the carrots.

The plump, black horse nuzzled her hand, as if to say "I'm really going to miss you too."

Holly joined them and Kitty stroked her shiny chestnut coat and gave her a carrot. "I hope I'll see you again soon," she said.

Holly tossed her mane and neighed. And although Kitty couldn't understand what she was saying now that she was in her human form, she felt certain the horse was saying, "I hope so too."

After they'd fed the carrots to the horses, Kitty, Max, and Daisy made their way to the barn. Star was curled up in a patch of sunlight in front of the barn doors, just as he'd been when Kitty first saw him. As soon as he saw them approaching his ears pricked up and he began to purr. Kitty picked up the big old tomcat and hugged him. "I'm going to miss you so much," she whispered in Star's ear. "But I promise I'll be back soon." The cat nuzzled his old, patched head against Kitty and meowed.

Daisy started leaping up excitedly and running around in circles chasing her tail. Star gave a big sigh, but Kitty could see that this time the old cat's eyes were twinkling and he was only pretending to be annoyed.

Uncle Greg offered to drive Grandma and Kitty to the station. As they left the farm, Kitty turned around in her seat to wave. In the distance, she spotted Star sitting on a window ledge with his tail dangling over. Daisy was yelping excitedly on the ground beneath, jumping up and down, trying to get

Star's tail. But every time the puppy jumped, Star flicked his tail just out of reach. Kitty giggled. Star and Daisy had finally found a way to play together! They really were a team now—and she was sure that Strawberry Lane Farm had seen its last mouse!

Kitty spent the whole train journey home excitedly telling Grandma about her adventures at Strawberry Lane Farm.

Grandma smiled when she heard that the farm was now mouse-free—thanks to Kitty! "I'm very proud of you, Kitty," she said warmly. "Just wait until you tell Misty and all your other cat friends at home about your adventure."

"Can I go see Misty tonight?" asked Kitty. She couldn't wait to see her friend.

"Of course!" replied Grandma. "I know she'll be desperate to see you, Kitty. We've all missed you!"

That evening, as soon as Kitty had unpacked, she raced over to Misty's house.

"You're back!" Misty purred excitedly as Kitty jumped down into her yard. "I've really missed you. Did you like the farm? What was the farm cat like?"

Kitty bumped foreheads with her friend and told her all about her adventure at Strawberry Lane Farm. Misty's blue eyes opened wide as she heard about Star and Daisy.

"You helped get rid of the mice at the farm *and* you helped a cat and a dog be friends?" she asked, amazed. "I can't believe it, Kitty! Just wait until the Cat Council hears about this. I don't think any Guardian has ever done that before. Everyone will be so impressed."

"Thanks, Misty!" Kitty meowed happily. She had to admit, she was very proud of how she'd helped her new friends at the farm. And she was looking forward to visiting them again soon. She wondered what her next challenge as Guardian would be. She couldn't wait to find out!

 MEET KITTY'S

Daisy is a
friendly border
collie puppy who
is new to life
on the farm.

Daisy

Holly

Holly is a big, gentle
farm horse. Holly is
always helping Seamus
get out of trouble.

Seamus is a
mischievous pony.
He is always hungry—
Seamus just loves
apples!

Seamus

FRIENDS

Star

Star is a little old farm cat. Star used to be the fastest cat around, but these days he needs a bit of help to catch mice!

Max is Kitty's cousin. He can be very shy, but he loves making new friends.

Max

Misty

Misty is a little gray kitten with a big imagination. Misty and Kitty are best friends!

FELINE FACTS

Here are some
fun facts about our
purrrfect animal friends
that you might like
to know . . .

1.

Cats and dogs can be taught
to **live together**
and be **friends**.

2.

Cats share 95% of their
DNA with **tigers**.

3.

Cats will chase **mice** just for fun!

4.

Cats make more than **100 different sounds** (dogs only make around 10).

5.

Adult cats only **meow** to communicate with humans.

Kitty's cat-friend Emerald is looking after two lost kittens, Frost and Snowdrop.

Can Kitty find their owner?

Read on for a glimpse of Kitty's next adventure . . .

"Well done, Misty!" whispered Kitty Kimura. "You're behaving so well!"

It was December, and Kitty had come to the local vet's with her best friend, Jenny, and Jenny's mom. It was time for Jenny's silver tabby cat, Misty, to have a check-up.

Kitty had watched as the vet, Mr. Singh, looked at Misty's eyes, ears, and teeth, then gently picked up each of her paws to glance at her claws and the soft pink pads underneath. "Everything looks fine," he told Jenny's mom. "It's very strange, though. Most cats get so nervous about these check-ups, but Misty is very relaxed!"

Kitty hid a smile as Misty gave a pleased, proud purr. She knew why Misty was so relaxed. That morning, Kitty had explained exactly what would happen during her check-up so Misty knew what to expect and wouldn't be frightened. Kitty was really glad she'd been able to help. After all, Misty was her friend too—although that was a secret.

A few months ago, Kitty had learned that she had an amazing gift. She could

turn into a cat! The only other person who knew about this was Kitty's grandma, who had the same special talent. Kitty had found it very strange to begin with, but now she loved her exciting secret—especially as cats were her favorite animals in the world. Now Kitty loved nothing more than transforming into a cat while her parents were fast asleep at night and exploring the village in her cat form—along with all her new cat friends, like Misty.

Kitty had even discovered that cats could speak to one another, just like people do. She also knew that cats could understand what people said, even though people couldn't understand a cat's meows.

"Misty's such a good, brave cat!" said Jenny, lifting her carefully from the vet's table and cuddling her soft gray fur. "Come on, let's get you home."

It had been very chilly for the last few days, so the girls wrapped up warmly in their winter coats and gloves before they set off for home. As they walked back to the street they lived on, with Jenny's mom behind them, something caught Kitty's eye. At the bottom of a fence were three small scratches in the shape of a triangle.

Someone's called a meeting of the Cat Council! Kitty thought excitedly. She glanced at Misty, curled up in Jenny's arms, and saw that her ears had pricked up and her whiskers were twitching. Misty had obviously spotted the symbol too.

Whenever any cat in the neighborhood had a problem or question or wanted to ask advice, they scratched the special triangle somewhere other cats would see it. Then everyone would come to a meeting of the Cat Council that night, in the woods close to Kitty's house.

I wonder who called this meeting? Kitty thought. *And I wonder what they want?*

That evening, while Kitty was eating dinner with her parents and grandma, her mom looked at her excitedly. "Kitty, guess what? Your dad and I have finally found a new assistant for the shop!"

Kitty's parents owned a shop that sold special Japanese things. They were often very busy, and traveled to Japan a few times a year to buy new things to sell. They'd been looking for a new assistant to help them out for ages. Kitty didn't mind them going away, though, because it meant she got to spend lots of time with her grandma, who lived with them.

"Her name is Nadia and she's going to start on Monday," said Kitty's dad. "We've invited her over for dinner soon, so you'll meet her then. She's very nice."

"That's good," said Kitty, nodding. But she wasn't really thinking about the shop. She was too curious about tonight's Cat Council meeting. Who could have called it? And why?

When dinner was finished and Kitty had helped clear the table, she gave a loud yawn. "I'm really sleepy," she said. "I think I might go to bed."

"But it's so early, Kitty," said her mom, giving her a cuddle. "You always used to love staying up late on Saturday nights, but you never seem to want to anymore."

"Yes, are you sure?" her dad said. "Your mom and I thought we could all watch a movie together tonight. You can choose it."

Kitty hesitated. She loved movie nights with her parents—especially as she and her dad liked acting out their

favorite scenes together afterwards. But she knew that she had to be at the Cat Council meeting tonight, no matter what. Grandma caught Kitty's eye and winked. She knew exactly why Kitty was so eager to go to bed early. Kitty's grandma was able to turn into a cat too!

"I really am tired," Kitty replied, pretending to yawn again and rubbing her eyes. "I've had so much homework this week."

"I could make popcorn," her mom suggested. "And hot chocolate with marshmallows. Your favorite!"

Those things did sound wonderful. Kitty's mouth watered at the thought of her mom's creamy, sweet hot chocolate. "Would it be okay if we did it tomorrow?" she said.

"Goodness, Kitty, you must be really tired to pass up hot chocolate with marshmallows!" her mom exclaimed. "Okay then, we'll do it tomorrow. Would you like me to come and tuck you in?"

"Oh no, I'm fine, honestly," Kitty said quickly. "Goodnight."

After giving her parents and grandma a kiss, Kitty ran up the stairs to her bedroom and closed the door. Finally, it was time to get ready!

As soon as she heard her parents going to bed, Kitty reached for the delicate silver necklace around her neck. The pendant had been a gift from Grandma. On it there was an engraving of a cat above some tiny, mysterious words. Very quietly, Kitty said the words aloud:

"Human hands to kitten paws,
Human fingers, kitten claws."

Right away, a strange feeling whirled through Kitty's body. She closed her eyes, smiling as a ticklish sensation bubbled from the tips of her toes to the top of her head. When it faded away, Kitty opened her eyes and blinked a few times. Then she swished her tail and twitched her whiskers. She was a cat!

Kitty loved being able to jump and leap in her cat form. With a happy meow, she sprang onto her bedside table, then onto the windowsill. She slipped out the open window and dropped onto the roof of the garden shed. A minute later, she was trotting along her street toward the woods.

When she reached the moonlit clearing where the Cat Council met, there was a group of cats waiting in a circle already. Everyone meowed a greeting to Kitty when they saw her arrive, and one by one they ran toward her to gently bump foreheads. Kitty had learned that this was how cats say hello.

Misty was there along with lots of Kitty's other friends, including an elegant blue-gray cat called Coco, a tiny Bengal kitten named Ruby, and a slender, snowy-white cat with bright green eyes and a matching green collar, who was called Emerald. Kitty took her place next to Tiger, a big, bossy but friendly ginger tomcat with stripes, who always led the Cat Council meetings.

"Welcome, everyone!" he said. A small black cat with a delicate white patch on her head slipped into her place in the circle right at the last moment. Kitty purred happily when she saw the older cat, whose name was Suki, arrive. Suki was a very special cat, especially to Kitty—because she was her grandma!

"Thank you all for coming," Tiger said. "Let's start by saying the Meow Vow together."

The cats chanted the special promise they all made at the beginning of every Cat Council meeting.

"We promise now,
  This solemn vow,
  To help somehow,
  When you meow."

Tiger nodded approvingly. "Before we begin, I wanted to give you all some important news," he said. "A fox has been spotted near the park. As you know, foxes can be dangerous, so please be careful!"

Ella Moonheart grew up telling fun and exciting stories to anyone who would listen. Now that she's an author, she's thrilled to be able to tell stories to so many more children with her Kitty's Magic books. Ella loves animals, but cats most of all! She wishes she could turn into one just like Kitty, but she's happy to just play with her pet cat, Nibbles—when she's not writing her books, of course!